FREDERICKA BERGER

The Green Bottle and the Silver Kite

Greenwillow Books, New York

First Edition 10 9 8 7 6 5 4 3 2 1

Library of Congress Cataloging-in-Publication Data

Berger, Fredericka
The green bottle and the silver kite / by Fredericka Berger.
p. cm.
Summary: While earning money to buy a special kite,
Phil annoys his sister and makes a new friend.
ISBN 0-688-11785-6
[1. Kites—Fiction. 2. Brothers and sisters—Fiction.
3. Beaches—Fiction.] I. Title.
PZ7.B4515Gr 1993
[Fic]—dc20 92-10073 CIP AC

To Conrad. And to Eric,
who once had a silver kite.

And thank you to the Hartzells.